Mairi's Mermaid

This edition published in Great Britain 2001 by Egmont Children's Books Ltd
First published in Great Britain 1994 by Methuen Children's Books
imprints of Egmont Children's Books Limited, a division of Egmont Holding Limited
239 Kensington High St, London W8 6SA
Published in hardback by Heinemann Library,
a division of Reed Educational and Professional Publishing Ltd,
by arrangement with Egmont Children's Books Limited.
Text copyright © Michael Morpurgo 1994
Illustrations copyright © Lucy Richards 2001
The author and illustrator have asserted their moral rights.
Paperback ISBN 0 7497 4272 0
Hardback ISBN 0 431 06976 X
5 7 9 10 8 6 4
A CIP catalogue record for this title is available from the British Library.
Printed in U. A. E.

Mairi's Mermaid

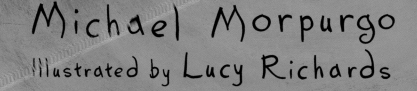

Michael Morpurgo

Illustrated by Lucy Richards

Blue Bananas

For Alan
M.M.

For Grandad Eric
and all my family
L.R.

Mairi still could not swim. She wished she could, but she just couldn't.

All the holidays she'd been trying, but every time she took her feet off the bottom she sank like a stone.

Her brother Robbie swam like a fish.
'It's easy,' he told her. 'You believe in
mermaids don't you? Well, just pretend
you're a mermaid, like this.'

He doesn't even have armbands.

Look at me!

He laughed and plunged headfirst into another towering green wave. Sometimes Robbie was a real show-off.

He's not as good as me.

Mairi's mother and father tried to help.

'It'll come' they said. 'You'll do it.'

But it didn't come and she didn't do it.

Mairi wanted to be miserable all

on her own.

She went to look for crabs in the rock
pools and tried to forget all about
swimming.

Soon she had collected five little crabs in
her bucket. They'd be her pets for the day.
Later she'd let them go and watch them
sidle away into the sea.

he water in the rock pool was warm from the sun. A shoal of silver fish darted round her legs. She could see a starfish and some sea anemones. 'Swimming looks so easy for them,' she thought.

That's a funny looking fish!

Suddenly something pinched her toe. She thought it might be a crab and jumped up. It was nothing. Maybe she had imagined it. But just to be sure, she decided not to dangle her feet again.

OUCH!

And then she heard a piping voice. It seemed at first to come from far away. She listened again. It came from deep down in the rock pool.

13

Mairi brushed aside the seaweed and there, glaring up at her, was a huge brown crab. In his great grasping claw was a fish, no bigger than her finger.

But then she saw it wasn't an ordinary fish. It was a fish with arms and hands, a fish with a head like her own and a mouth that spoke. It was a little mermaid.

Mairi was not at all afraid of crabs, however big they were. She picked the crab out of the water and shook him and shook him.

The little mermaid dropped into the pool and disappeared.

For a moment there was no sign of her.
Then a small head bobbed up. 'Thank
you, oh, thank you,' the mermaid said.

Are
you real?

Mairi never knew mermaids could be
this small. She wasn't sure mermaids
were even real.

'Help me, please,' said the mermaid.

'I went off on my own and I got stuck in this pool. Then that great big horrible crab caught me. He was going to eat me up!'

Of course I'm real!

Mairi would *so* like to have kept her as a pet for the day, but she knew what she had to do.

Mairi carried the little mermaid carefully over the rocks and down to the sea. Then she opened her hands, and let the mermaid go. But the mermaid wouldn't go.

I must get home.

Little Mermaid, your mother is worried.

'No, no!' cried the little mermaid clutching her thumb. 'Not here. The waves will smash me against the rocks. Take me out to that rock over there. Please! That's where we all live, in a big cave under that rock.'

'But I can't swim,' said Mairi.

21

'I'll tell you what,' Mairi said. I'll take you as far as I can walk, but I can't go out of my depth.'

She stepped into the sea and waded out until the sea water came as high as her knees . . .

It's not far.

as high as her waist . . .

as high as her neck . . .

Suddenly a great wave came rolling in and lifted her right off her feet and when she came down there was no sandy bottom under her feet, no bottom at all.

Hold on Mairi!

Oh!

Mairi kicked and
splashed and the
seawater came right
into her mouth.

Take a deep breath!

25

'It's all right,' said the little mermaid.

'You're swimming!'

And when Mairi kicked again, she did
not sink. She was swimming! She was!

I'm not
sinking!

She lifted her chin and paddled through the sea, keeping her mouth tightly closed. Together, Mairi and the little mermaid swam to the rock.

You're swimming!

Not bad, for someone with only two legs.

Home safe and sound.

They were almost there when Mairi felt an arm around her waist, then another and another. The sea around her was suddenly full of mermaids.

The little mermaid was clinging to her mother's hair.

Who's that with her?

She's back!

Then Mairi felt the rock beneath her feet

and she could stand.

The little mermaid was telling everyone

her story. 'Look what the

crab did to my tail,'

she said.

'Maybe it'll teach you not to go off like that,' said her mother. 'I've told you and told you. If it hadn't have been for this girl.' She smiled at Mairi. 'How can we ever thank you?' she said.

Mairi shook the crab!

And Mairi had a sudden idea.

'You couldn't teach me how to swim, could you?' she asked. 'I mean, like you do, like mermaids do.'

Don't be afraid! Follow us.

First they taught her how to lie on the water and float. Mairi could feel the water holding her up!

Doggy

paddle was

next . . .

then

breaststroke . . .

then crawl . . .

backstroke . . .

butterfly . . .

They even taught her to swim underwater!

Mairi wasn't afraid of the sea anymore.

She loved it!

Wow!

This is our home.

Pull up a shell.

Some time later Robbie was waiting for the next really big wave to come in, waiting for just the right one to dive into. 'Look at this one!' he cried as a great green wave came curling in.

It's the biggest yet!

He was just about to dive into it when he saw what looked like a seal swimming along the crest of the wave.

Bye Mairi!

You swim like a mermaid now.

Like a fish, you mean!

But it wasn't a seal, it was Mairi. It was

Mairi swimming!

As she swept past him, his mouth opened

in astonishment and the seawater swept in.

'You can swim!' he spluttered.

Mairi's mother and father came running

down to the water's edge.

Look
at me!

'You can swim!' they cried.

'Course I can,' she said. 'It's easy.

I just pretended I was a mermaid.'

We knew you'd do it!